J 978.7 GAL
Galiano, Dean.
Wyoming

S0-EAW-769

WITHDRAWN

AVON PUBLIC LIBRARY
BOX 977/200 BENCHMARK RD.
AVON, CO 81620

EAGLE VALLEY LIBRARY DISTRICT

1 06 0003689640

PowerKids Readers:

The Bilingual Library of the United States of America™

WYOMING

DEAN GALIANO

TRADUCCIÓN AL ESPAÑOL: MARÍA CRISTINA BRUSCA

The Rosen Publishing Group's
PowerKids Press™ & **Editorial Buenas Letras**™
New York

Bilingual Edition
English/Spanish
Edición bilingüe

Published in 2006 by The Rosen Publishing Group, Inc.
29 East 21st Street, New York, NY 10010

Copyright © 2006 by The Rosen Publishing Group, Inc.

All rights reserved. No part of this book may be reproduced in any form without permission in writing from the publisher, except by a reviewer.

First Edition

Photo Credits: Cover © John Elk III/Lonely Planet Images; p. 5 © Joe Sohm/The Image Works; p. 7 © 2002 Geoatlas; p. 9 © Robert Everts/Getty Images; pp. 11, 15, 31 (Buffalo Bill, Taylor Ross, Geyser) © Bettmann/Corbis; p. 13 © North Wind Picture Archives; pp. 17, 31 (Ranches) © Joel Bennett/Peter Arnold, Inc., p. 19 © Bobby Model/National Geographic Image Collection; p. 21 © Paul Chesley/Getty Images; p. 23 © Roy Rainford/Getty Images; pp. 25, 30 (Capital) © Mary Steinbacher/Getty Images; p. 26 © Bill Ross/Corbis; p. 30 (Indian Paintbrush) © D. Robert & Lorri Franz/Corbis; p. 30 (Western Meadowlark) © Joe McDonald/Corbis; p. 30 (Plains Cottonwood) © Joseph Sohm; ChromoSohm Inc./Corbis; p. 30 (Jade) © Vaughan Fleming/Photo Researchers, Inc.; p. 31 (Bridger) Library of Congress Prints and Photographs Division; p. 31 (Warren) © Picture History; p. 31 (Simpson) © Steven G. Smith/Corbis/Corbis; p. 31 (Cheney) © William Philpott/Reuters/Corbis; p. 31 (Pelts) © Douglas Peebles/Corbis

Library of Congress Cataloging-in-Publication Data

Galiano, Dean.
Wyoming / Dean Galiano ; traducción al español, María Cristina Brusca. — 1st ed.
    p. cm. — (The bilingual library of the United States of America)
Includes bibliographical references and index.
ISBN 1-4042-3116-1 (library binding)
1. Wyoming—Juvenile literature. I. Title. II. Series.
F761.3.G355 2006
978.7—dc22
                                            2005032642

Manufactured in the United States of America

Due to the changing nature of Internet links, Editorial Buenas Letras has developed an online list of Web sites related to the subject of this book. This site is updated regularly. Please use this link to access the list:

http://www.buenasletraslinks.com/ls/wyoming

AVON PUBLIC LIBRARY
BOX 977/200 BENCHMARK RD.
AVON, CO 81620

Contents

Contenido

Welcome to Wyoming

Wyoming became a state on July 10, 1890. The words "equal rights" are found on Wyoming's state seal. This means that all people in Wyoming have the same rights.

Bienvenidos a Wyoming

El 10 de julio de 1890 se creó el estado de Wyoming. En el escudo del estado dice "igualdad de derechos". Ésto significa que en Wyoming todas las personas tienen los mismos derechos.

Wyoming Flag and State Seal

Bandera y escudo de Wyoming

Wyoming Geography

Wyoming is located in the Rocky Mountain area of the United States. Wyoming borders the states of Montana, Idaho, Utah, Colorado, Nebraska, and South Dakota.

Geografía de Wyoming

Wyoming se encuentra en la región de las montañas Rocosas. Wyoming linda con los estados de Montana, Idaho, Utah, Colorado, Nebraska y Dakota del Sur.

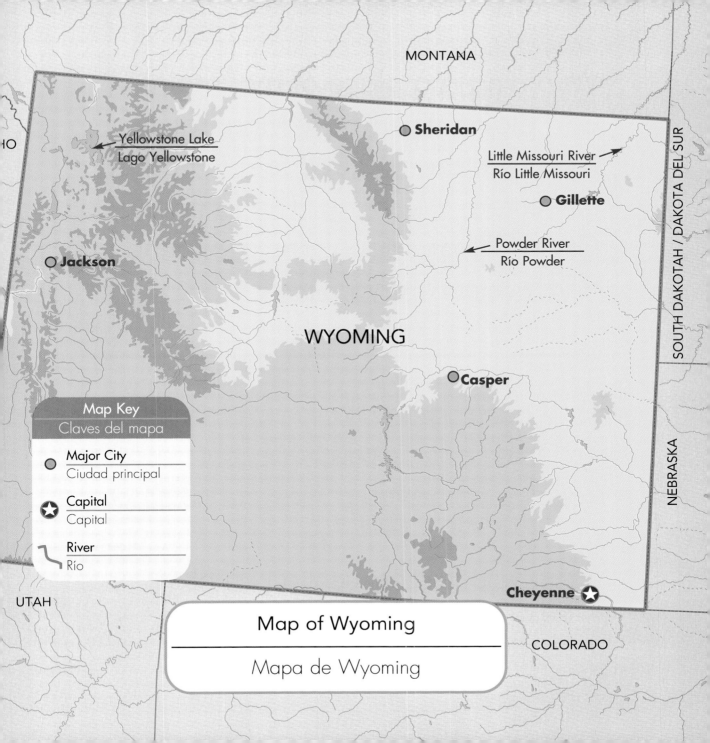

MONTANA

Yellowstone Lake
Lago Yellowstone

● Sheridan

Little Missouri River
Río Little Missouri

● Gillette

Powder River
Río Powder

● Jackson

SOUTH DAKOTA / DAKOTA DEL SUR

WYOMING

● Casper

NEBRASKA

Map Key
Claves del mapa

● Major City
Ciudad principal

★ Capital
Capital

River
Río

Cheyenne ★

UTAH

COLORADO

Map of Wyoming

Mapa de Wyoming

Wyoming is a place of mountains and plains. The Rocky Mountains rise more than 13,000 feet (3,962 m) in western Wyoming. The famous Grand Teton Mountains are found in northwestern Wyoming.

En Wyoming hay llanuras y montañas. En el oeste del estado, las montañas Rocosas se elevan a más de 13,000 pies (3,900 m). Las famosas montañas Gran Teton se encuentran en el noroeste de Wyoming.

Jackson Lake In Grand Teton National Park

Lago Jackson en el Parque Nacional Gran Teton

Wyoming History

In 1807, John Colter visited the Yellowstone area. Colter told people about the geysers and boiling mud pits he saw there. In 1872, President Grant made Yellowstone the first national park.

Historia de Wyoming

En 1807, John Colter visitó la región de Yellowstone. Colter describió los géiseres y piletas de barro hirviente que había visto allí. En 1872, el presidente Grant creó el primer parque nacional en Yellowstone.

Old Faithful Geyser in Yellowstone National Park

Géiser Old Faithful en el Parque Nacional Yellowstone

From 1825 to 1840, fur trappers gathered yearly at the Green River Rendezvous. "Rendezvous" means a place where people meet. Trappers traded beaver pelts for food and other supplies.

De 1825 a 1840, los tramperos se reunieron todos los años en Green River Rendezvous. "Rendezvous" significa lugar donde la gente se reúne. Allí, los tramperos cambiaban sus pieles de castor por comida y otras provisiones.

Native American Trapper

Trampero nativoamericano

Nellie Tayloe Ross was elected governor of Wyoming in 1924. Ross was the first woman governor of a U.S. state. Later she also served as the first woman director of the U.S. Mint.

Nellie Tayloe Ross fue elegida gobernadora de Wyoming en 1924. Ross fue la primera mujer en gobernar un estado. Fue también la primera mujer en dirigir la Casa de la Moneda de E.U.A.

Nellie Tayloe Ross

AVON PUBLIC LIBRARY
BOX 977/200 BENCHMARK RD.
AVON, CO 81620

Living in Wyoming

Ranching is an important activity in Wyoming. Wyoming has more than 9,000 ranches. The ranches are very large. Cattle and sheep are raised on the ranches.

La vida en Wyoming

La ganadería es una actividad muy importante en Wyoming. Wyoming tiene más de 9,000 ranchos. Los ranchos son muy grandes. En ellos se crían vacas y ovejas.

Cowboys Rounding Up Cows

Vaqueros arreando ganado

Rodeo is the state sport of Wyoming. Cowboys and cowgirls compete in events such as bull riding. The Cheyenne Frontier Days is the largest outdoor rodeo in the world.

El rodeo es el deporte del estado de Wyoming. Vaqueros y vaqueras compiten en eventos como la monta de toros. El rodeo Cheyenne Frontier Days es el rodeo al aire libre más grande del mundo.

A Cowboy Competes in a Rodeo

Vaquero compitiendo en un rodeo

Wyoming Today

Mining is Wyoming's most important business. Wyoming produces more coal than any other state does. Wyoming also produces large amounts of oil and natural gas.

Wyoming, hoy

La minería es el negocio más importante de Wyoming. Wyoming produce más carbón que cualquier otro estado. También produce grandes cantidades de petróleo y gas natural.

Mining in Rock Springs, Wyoming

Minería en Rock Springs, Wyoming

Yellowstone and Grand Teton are world-famous national parks. Millions of people visit the parks each year to see their natural beauty. Many wild animals such as bears and bison live in the parks.

Los parques nacionales Yellowstone y Grand Teton son famosos en todo el mundo. Cada año, millones de personas visitan estos parques para ver sus bellezas naturales. En los parques viven muchos animales salvajes, como osos y bisontes.

Bison in Yellowstone National Park
Bisontes en el Parque Nacional Yellowstone

Cheyenne is the capital of Wyoming and its largest city. The city was named after the Cheyenne Native American nation. Other important cities in Wyoming are Casper and Laramie.

Cheyenne es la ciudad más grande de Wyoming y también su capital. El nombre de esta ciudad honra a la nación indígena Cheyenne. Casper y Laramie son ciudades importantes de Wyoming.

Capitol Building in Cheyenne, Wyoming

Capitolio en Cheyenne, Wyoming

Activity:
Let's Draw Devil's Tower
Devil's Tower is America's first national monument.

Actividad:
Dibujemos la Torre del Diablo
La Torre del Diablo es el primer monumento nacional de E.U.A.

1

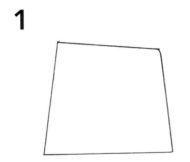

Start by drawing the shape shown. Angle the two vertical lines in toward the top of the shape.

Comienza por trazar una forma como la del modelo, de manera que las líneas verticales se cierren un poco hacia la parte de arriba.

2

Use the guide to draw the shape of the tower.

Dibuja la forma de la torre siguiendo las líneas de guía.

3

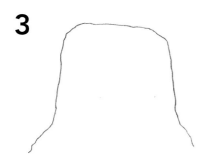

Erase the extra lines.

Borra las líneas sobrantes.

4

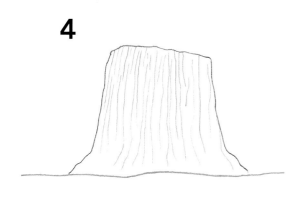

Draw a wavy line below the tower for the land. Add wavy lines in the tower.

Traza una línea ondulada bajo la torre para representar la tierra. Agrega otras líneas onduladas a la torre.

5

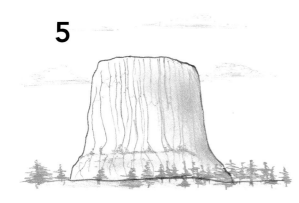

Draw the trees and the clouds. Add shading and detail.

Dibuja los árboles y las nubes. Agrega sombras y detalles.

Timeline

Cronología

John Colter enters the area of Yellowstone National Park.	**1807**	John Colter entra en la región del parque Nacional Yellowstone.
Beginning of the fur trade rendezvous period.	**1825**	Con el trueque de pieles comienza el período rendevouz.
Gold is discovered in the South Pass district.	**1842**	Se descubre oro en el distrito de South Pass.
Jim Bridger discovers Bridger Pass, the future route of the Union Pacific Railroad.	**1850**	Jim Bridger descubre Bridger Pass, futura ruta del ferrocarril Union Pacific.
Wyoming Territory is created.	**1868**	Se crea el Territorio de Wyoming.
Wyoming becomes the forty-fourth state.	**1890**	Wyoming se convierte en el estado número cuarenta y cuatro.
Nellie Tayloe Ross becomes the first woman governor in the United States.	**1925**	Nellie Tayloe Ross llega a ser la primera mujer gobernadora de un estado de los Estados Unidos.

Wyoming Events

Eventos en Wyoming

January
Wyoming Windy City Quilt Festival
in Casper

Enero
Festival Wyoming Windy City Quilt,
en Casper

February
Crystal Classic Ice Sculpting
in Green River

Febrero
Concurso de esculturas de hielo Crystal
Classic, en Green River

March
4-H Carnival in Casper

Marzo
Carnaval 4-H, en Casper

April
Cardboard Box Derby in Jackson

Abril
Carrera de autos Carboard Box, en Jackson

May
High School Rodeo Competition
in Casper

Mayo
Competencia de rodeo de la escuela
secundaria, en Casper

June
College National Finals Rodeo
in Casper
Flaming Gorge Days in Green River

Junio
Finales universitarias nacionales de rodeo,
en Casper
Días Flaming Gorge, en Green River

July
Cheyenne Frontier Days in Cheyenne

Julio
Días de la frontera de Cheyenne,
en Cheyenne

October
Fall Harvest Festival in Buffalo

Octubre
Festival de la cosecha de otoño, en Buffalo

November
Native American Craft Show
in Lander

Noviembre
Exposición de artesanías
nativoamericanas, en Lander

29

Wyoming Facts/Datos sobre Wyoming

Population
501,242

Población
501,242

Capital
Cheyenne

Capital
Cheyenne

State Motto
"Equal Rights"

Lema del estado
"Igualdad de derechos"

State Flower
Indian paintbrush

Flor del estado
Hierba de conejo

State Bird
Western meadowlark

Ave del estado
Pradero Occidental

State Nickname
The Equality State

Mote del estado
Estado de la igualdad

State Tree
Plains cottonwood

Árbol del estado
Álamo de los llanos

State Song
"Wyoming"

Canción del estado
"Wyoming"

State Gemstone
Jade

Piedra preciosa
Jade

Famous Wyomingites/Wyominguitas famosos

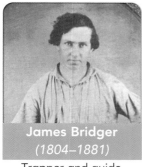

James Bridger
(1804–1881)

Trapper and guide

Guía y trampero

Francis E. Warren
(1844–1929)

Governor

Gobernador

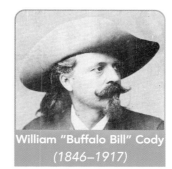

William "Buffalo Bill" Cody
(1846–1917)

Entertainer

Presentador de espectáculos

Nellie Tayloe Ross
(1876–1977)

Governor

Gobernadora

Alan K. Simpson
(1931–   )

U.S. Senator

Senador de E.U.A.

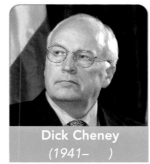

Dick Cheney
(1941–   )

Vice President of the United States

Vicepresidente de E.U.A.

Words to Know/Palabras que debes saber

border

frontera

geyser

géiser

pelts

pieles

ranches

ranchos

31

Here are more books to read about Wyoming:
Otros libros que puedes leer sobre Wyoming:

In English/En inglés:

C Is for Cowboy: A Wyoming Alphabet
by Eugene Gagliano
Sleeping Bear Press, 2003

How to Draw Vermont's Sights and Symbols
by Stephanie True Peters
PowerKids Press, 2002

Words in English: 321   Palabras en español: 356

Index

Índice